The Little Prince

COLORING BOOK

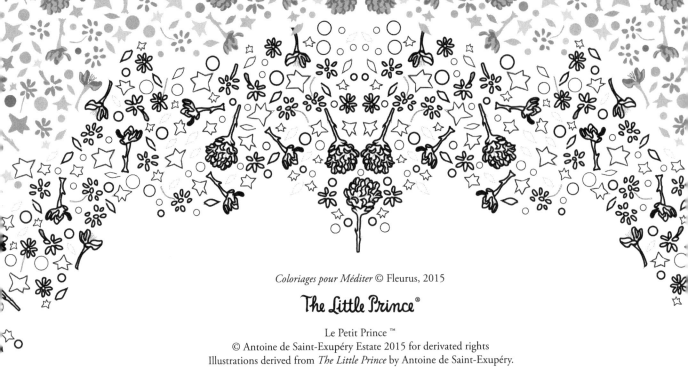

Coloriages pour Méditer © Fleurus, 2015

The Little Prince®

Le Petit Prince ™
© Antoine de Saint-Exupéry Estate 2015 for derivated rights
Illustrations derived from *The Little Prince* by Antoine de Saint-Exupéry.

Some text was previously published by Harcourt in *The Little Prince,* Copyright © 1943,
© renewed 1971 by Antoine de Saint-Exupéry Estate. English translation copyright © 2000 by Richard Howard.

ISBN: 978-0-544-79258-6

Houghton Mifflin Harcourt
222 Berkeley Street
Boston, Massachusetts 02116
www.hmhco.com

English edition packaging by Carol Chu

Manufactured in the United States of America
DOW 10 9 8 7 6 5 4 3 2 1
4500563747

BEAUTIFUL IMAGES FOR YOU
TO COLOR AND ENJOY

The Little Prince

COLORING BOOK

It's **hard**
to take up drawing again

at my **age.**

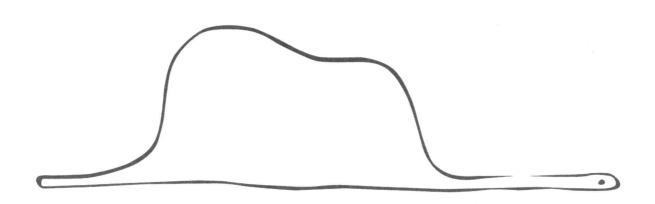

On the Little Prince's planet, there were—as on all planets—
good plants and bad plants. The good plants come from good seeds
and bad plants come from bad seeds.

If a child comes to you, if he laughs, if he has golden hair,

if he doesn't answer your questions, you'll know who he is.

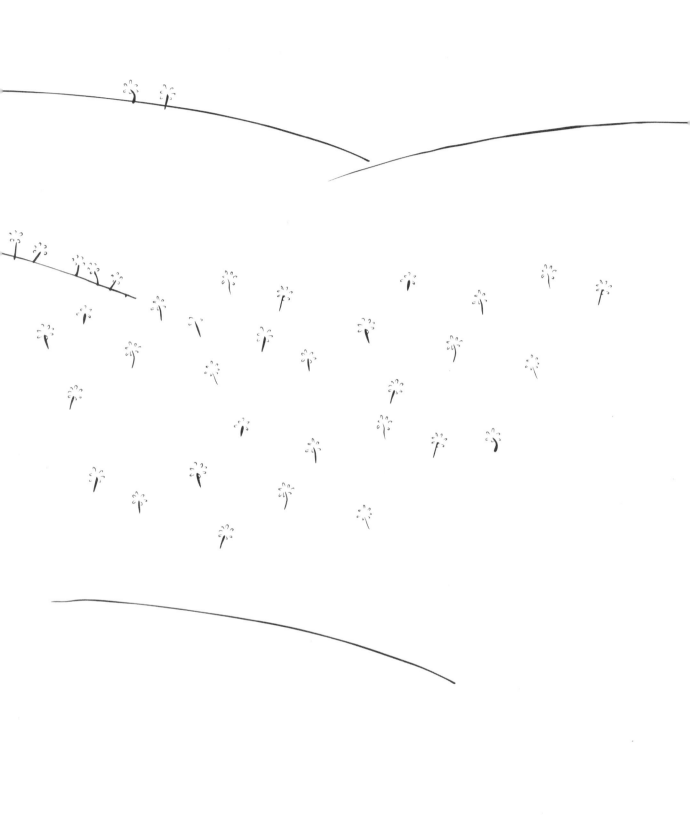

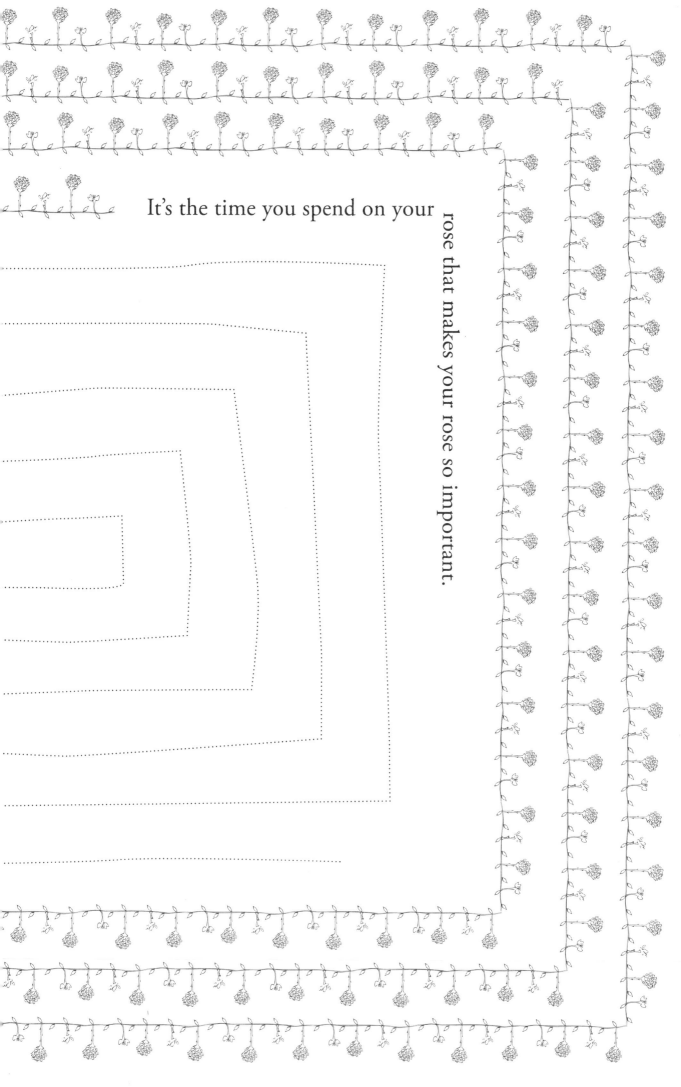

It's the time you spend on your rose that makes your rose so important.

I really like sunsets. Let's go look at one now.

You know, when you are feeling sad, sunsets are wonderful.

If you want a friend, tame me!

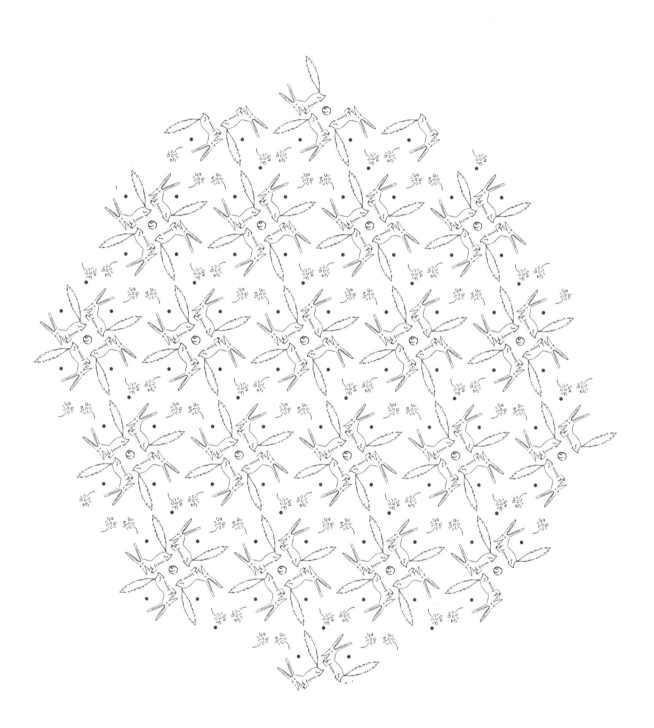

"Let's be friends," said the prince. "I'm lonely."

Once upon a time
there was a little prince who lived
on a planet hardly bigger than he was,
and who needed a friend . . .

Straight ahead, you can't go

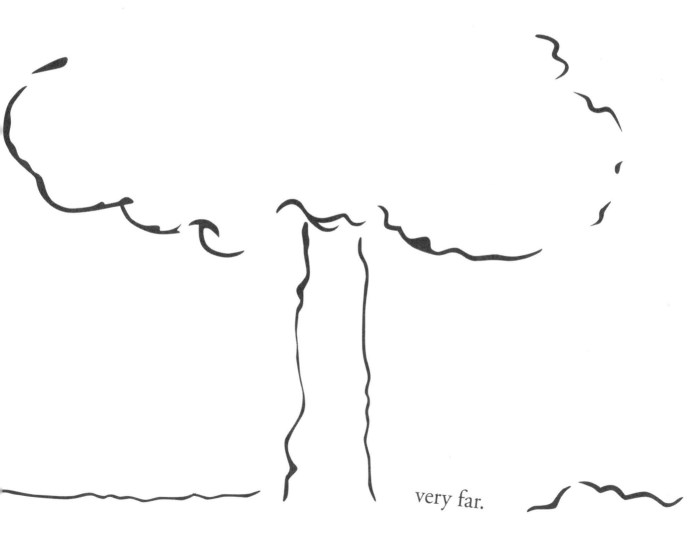

very far.

One sees clearly only from the heart.

Anything essential is invisible to the eye.

One sees clearly only from the heart.

Anything essential is invisible to the eye.

For some who are travelers, the stars are guides.

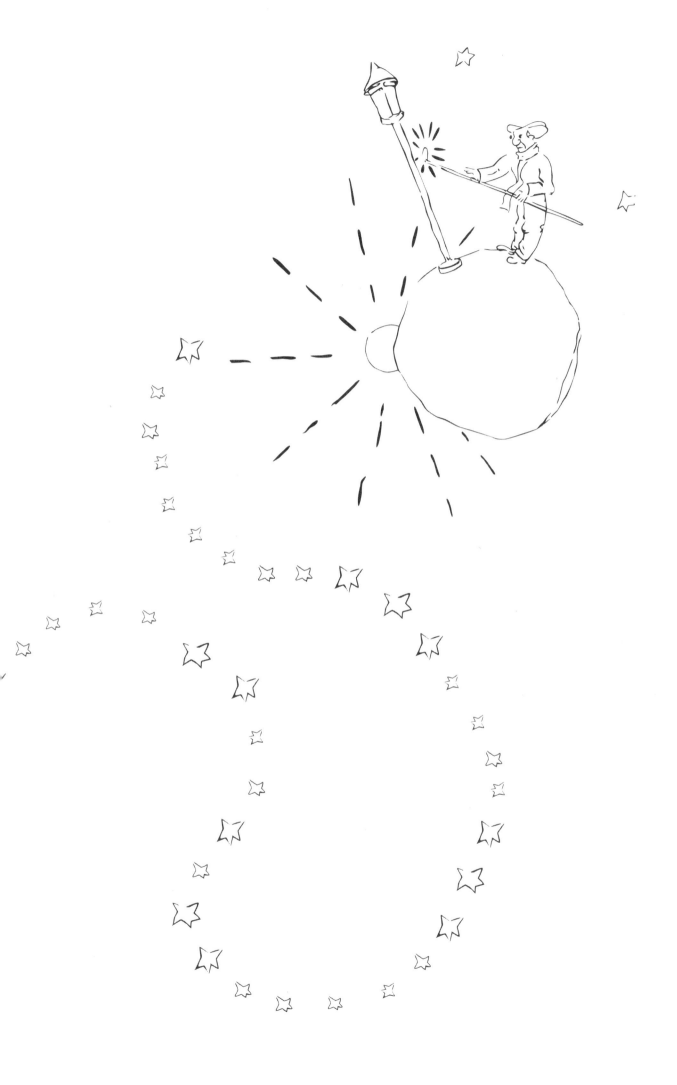

On the Little Prince's planet there had always been very simple flowers . . . that got in no one's way.

When one tries to be witty,
one sometimes wanders a little
from the truth.

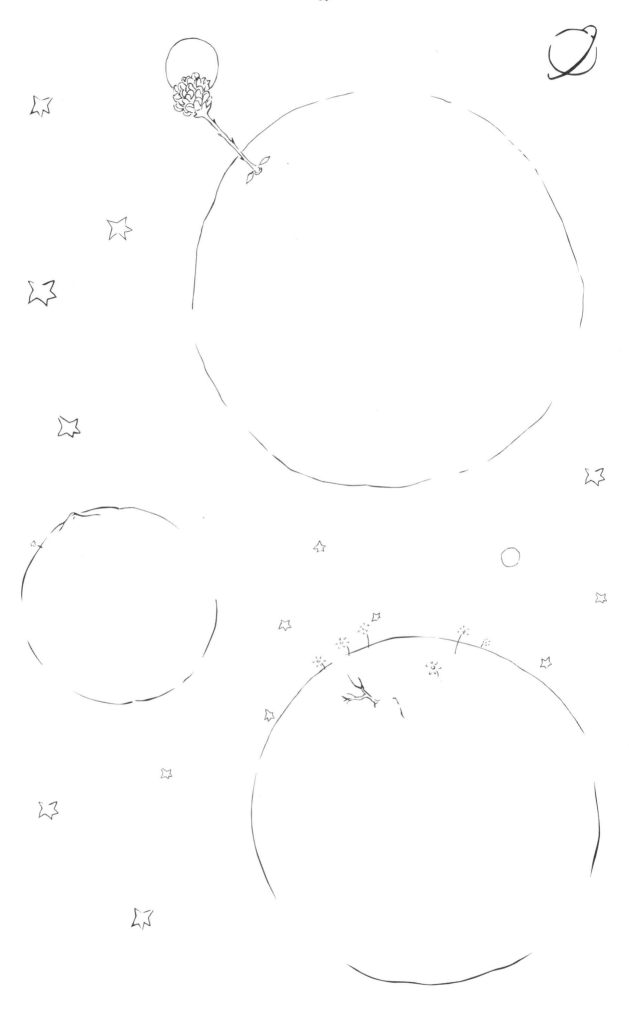

In order to make his escape, I believe he took advantage of a migration of wild birds.

The Little Prince crossed the desert and

encountered only one flower.

People have no roots, which hampers them a good deal. The wind can blow them away.

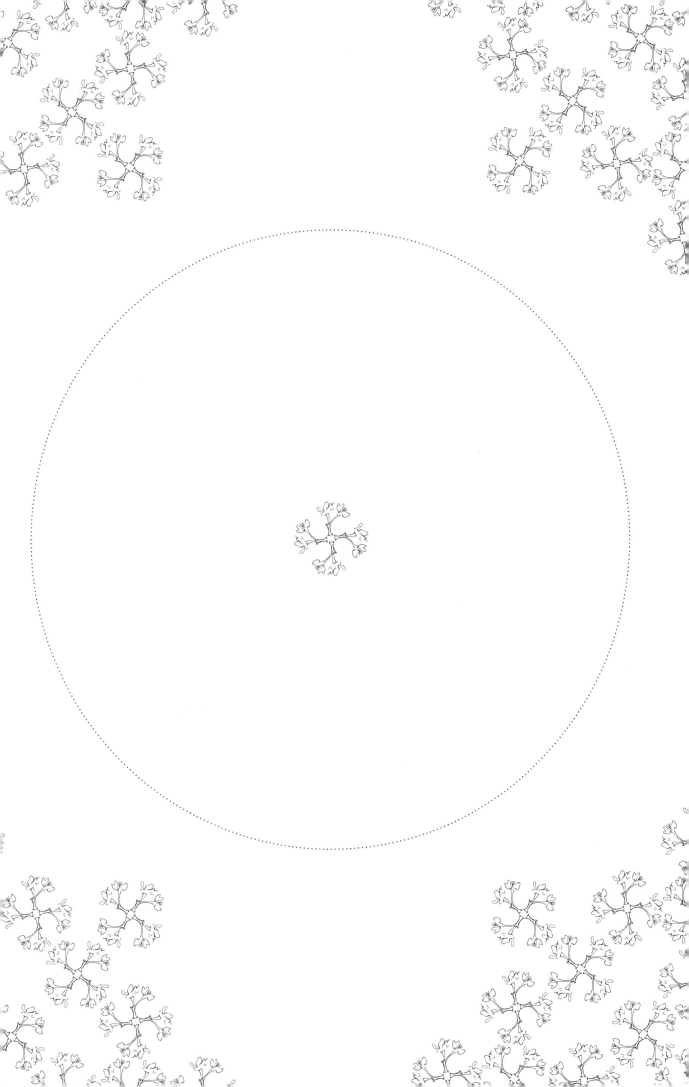

On Earth, one sees all kinds of things.

I like to listen to the stars at night.

It's like five hundred million bells . . .

Please . . . draw me a sheep . . .

My flower's
up there somewhere . . .

Sometimes there is no harm in putting off a piece of work until another day.

But when it is a matter of baobabs, that always means a catastrophe.

Flowers are *ephemeral*,
which means threatened by
imminent disappearance.

You'll be the only boy in the world for me. I'll be the only fox in the world for you.

I thought I was rich because I had just one flower,

and all I own is an ordinary rose.

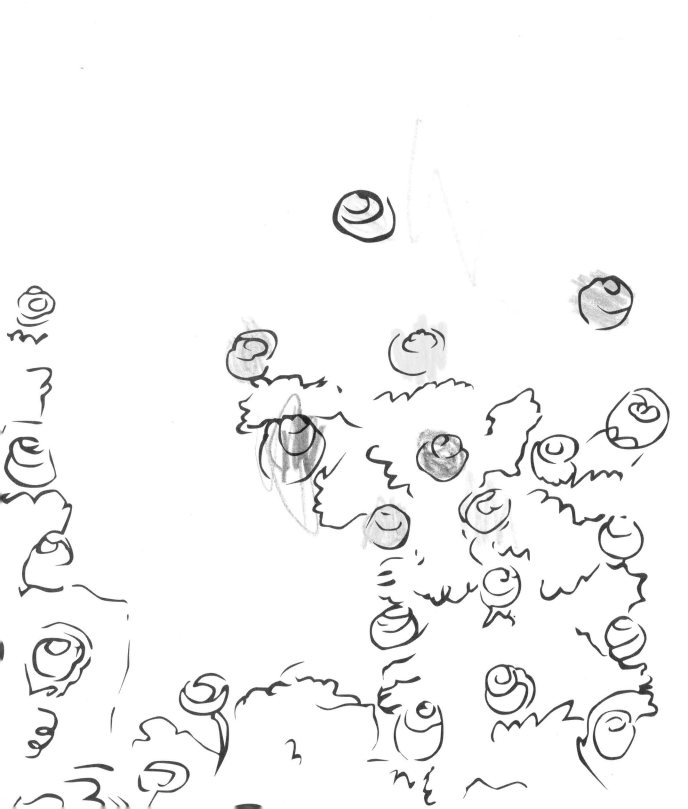

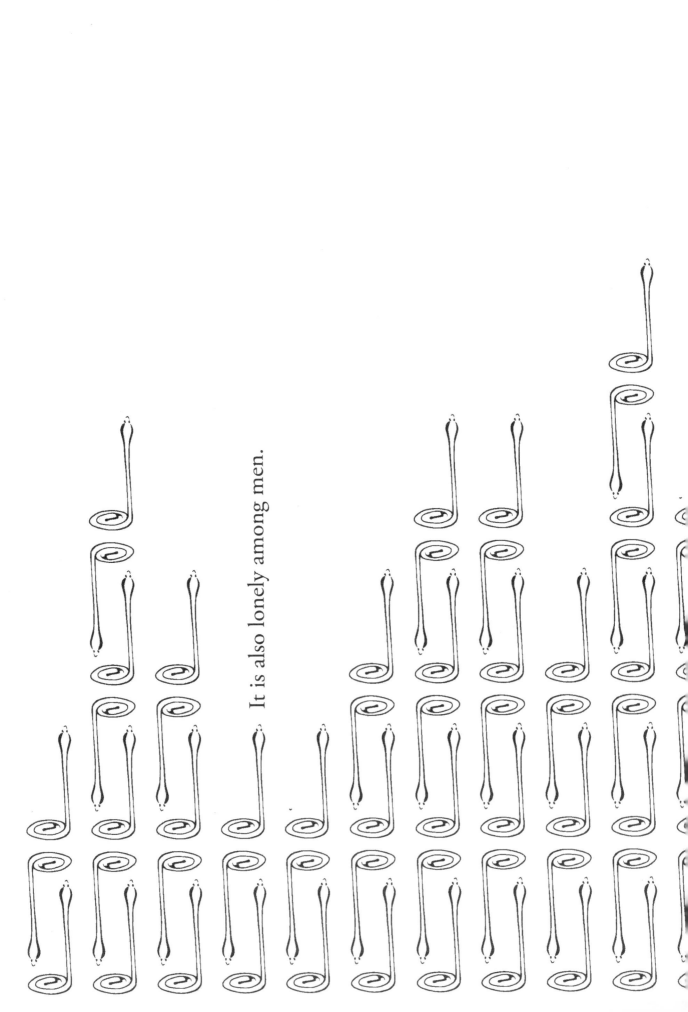

It is also lonely among men.

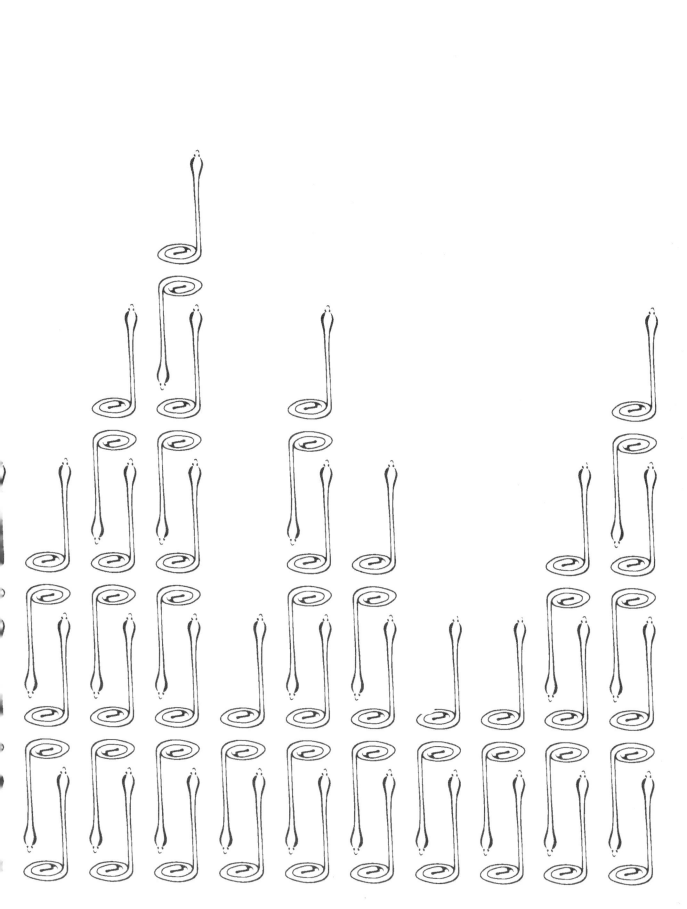

It's too small,
where I live,

for me to show you
where my star is.

It's better
that way.

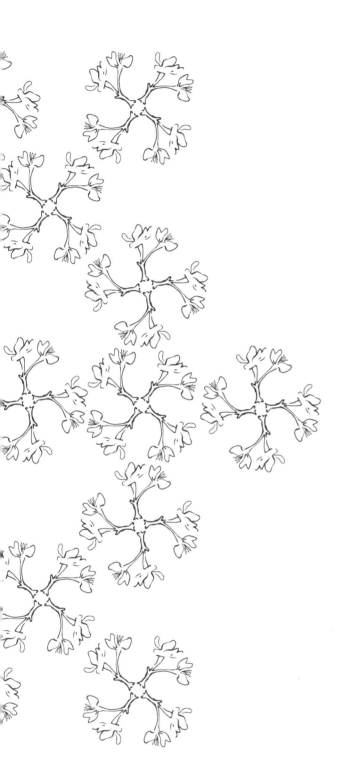

Words are the source
of misunderstandings.

It's all a great
mystery.

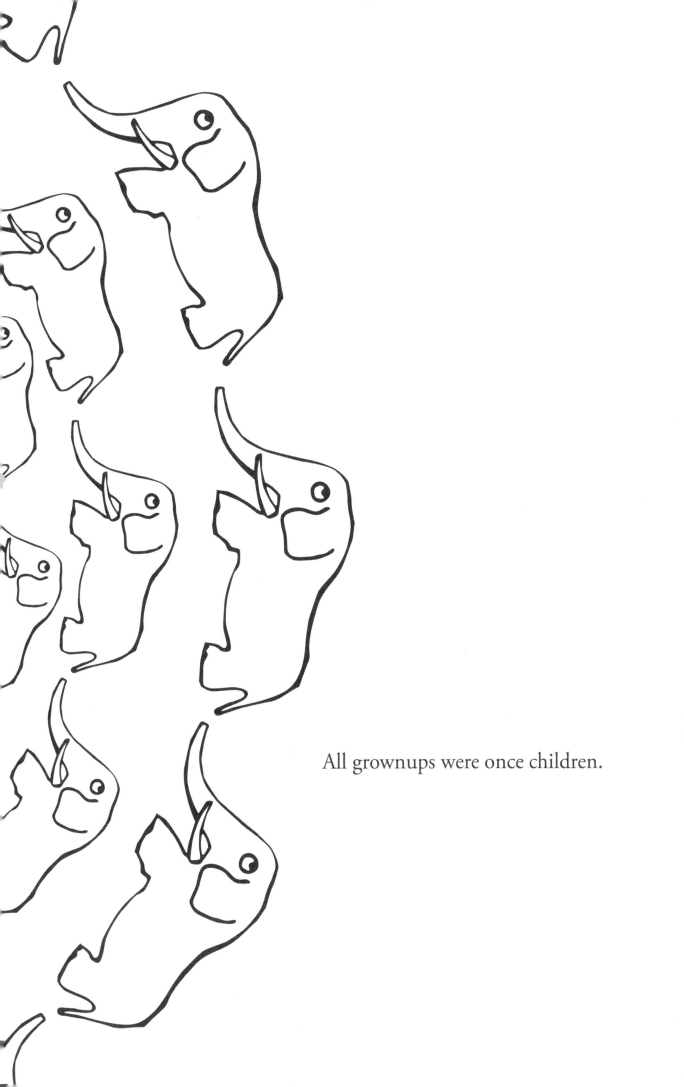

All grownups were once children.

A sheep eats
whatever it finds.

"Anyone I touch I can send back

to the land from which he came," said the snake.

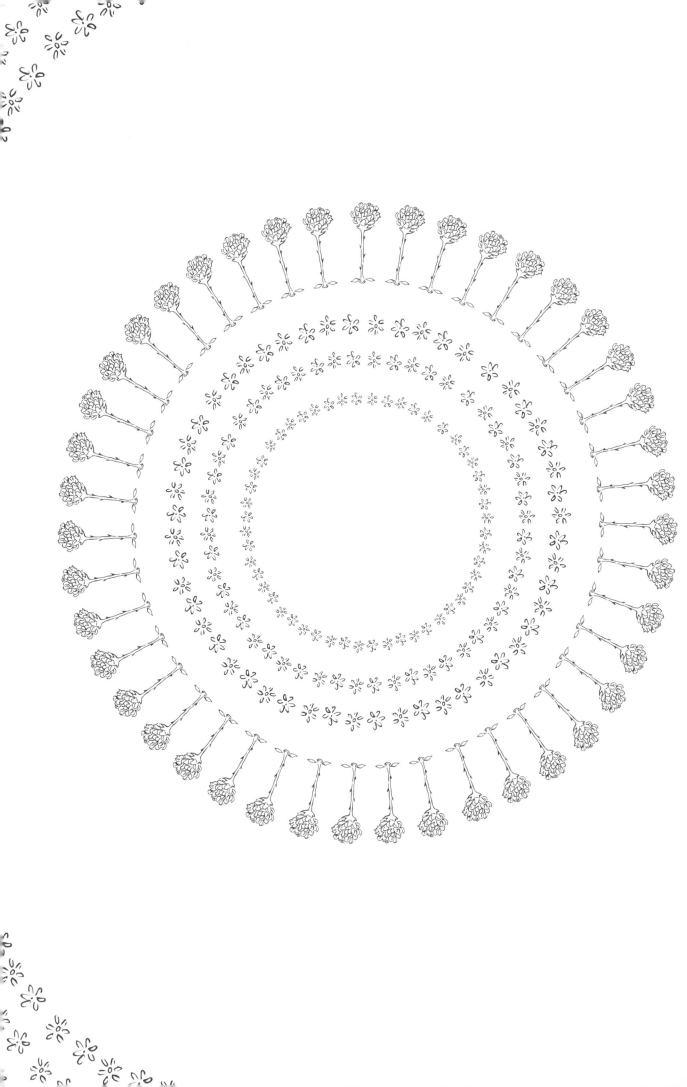

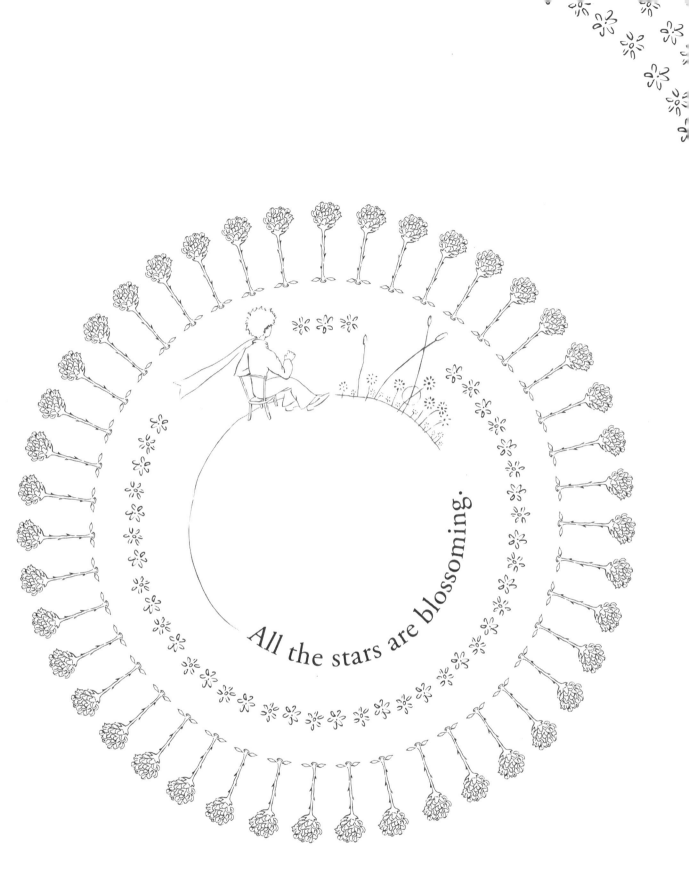

All the stars are blossoming.

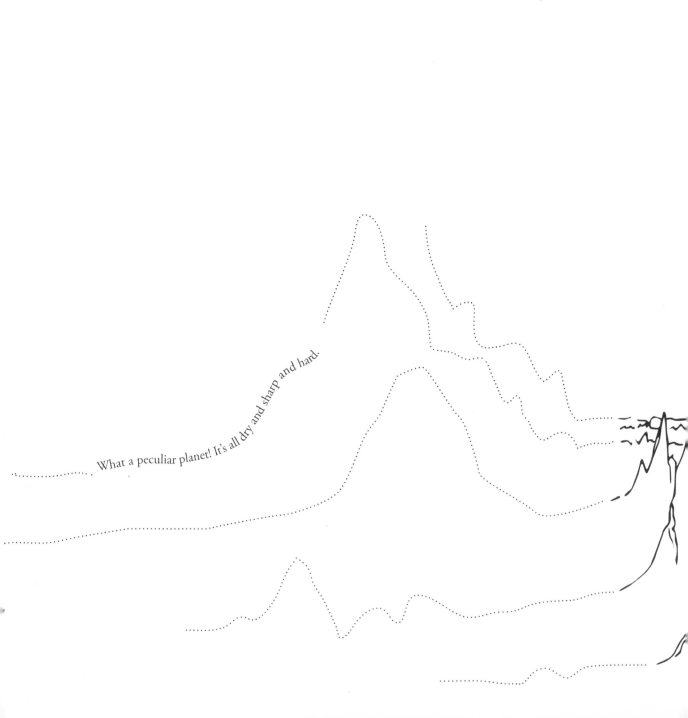

What a peculiar planet! It's all dry and sharp and hard.

We see nothing,
we hear nothing.
And something shines
in the silence.

When the
time to leave
was near,
the fox was ready
to weep.

And he lay down in the grass and wept.

And he lay down in the grass and wept.

If you love a flower
that lives on a star,
it's good at night
to look at the sky.

The stars are beautiful

because of a flower you don't see.

If you tame me,
we will need
each other.

You become responsible
for what you have tamed.

Only the children know what they are looking for.

We write of eternal things.

Your memories are beautiful.

We can't always see what is most important.

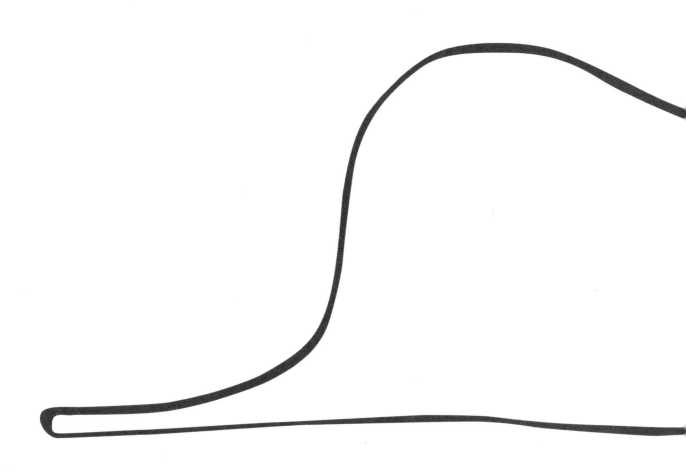

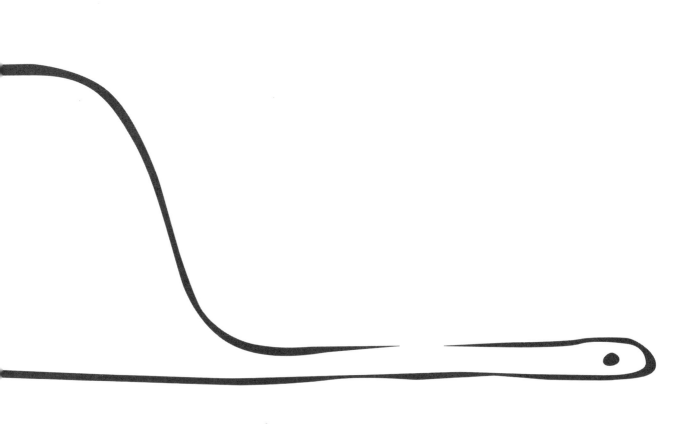